To ....

Welcome aboard the
Spooky Express!

From ....

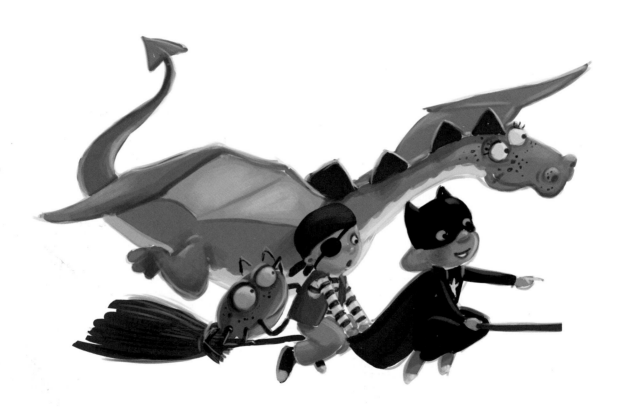

THE SPOOKY EXPRESS

MICHIGAN

A Halloween Thrill Ride

For Denise Shekleton.

Visit the author's website! http://ericjames.co.uk

Written by Eric James
Illustrated by Marcin Piwowarski
Designed by Sarah Allen

Published by Sourcebooks Jabberwocky, an imprint of Sourcebooks, Inc.
P.O. Box 4410, Naperville, Illinois 60567-4410
(630) 961-3900
Fax: (630) 961-2168
jabberwockykids.com

Date of Production: May 2017
Run Number: HTW_PO130117
Printed and bound in China (GD)
10 9 8 7 6 5 4 3 2 1

THE SPOOKY EXPRESS
MICHIGAN

Written by Eric James
Illustrated by Marcin Piwowarski

sourcebooks
jabberwocky

We were out trick-or-treating,
my best friend and I,
when we saw a huge shape
swooping down from the sky.

It circled around us
on train tracks of mist,
then it came to a stop,
and its large pistons hissed.

What a marvelous train,
engine black as the night!
All its carriages glowed
with a ghostly green light.

ALIENS IN ANN ARBOR

MAY'S CANDY

CINEMA

Tickets

OPEN

And we both held our breath
when its loud whistle blew,
for the sound that it made
was a ghastly *Woo-wooooo!*

He said, "Spooky Express!
Hop aboard. Take a ride!"
"How exciting!" we thought,
and we climbed up inside.

We looked all around.
What a wonderful sight!
We saw ghosts to our left.
We saw ghouls to our right.

There were mummies in tatters,
and witches in hats,
and ogres, and werewolves,
and vampire bats!

There were **big** trolls
from Saginaw
towering in size,
and aliens from Holland
with bright, bulging **eyes**.

KALAMAZOO

TRAVERSE CITY

BATTLE CREEK

ISHPEMING

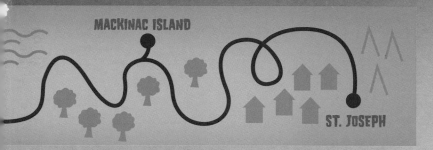

A voice on the speaker said,
"Please hold on tight!"
Then the train gave a lurch
and launched into the night.

We glided along
through a dark stormy sky.
The gardens in downtown
Grand Rapids *whizzed* by.

We zipped over Sterling Heights,
saw its bright lights,
and looked down on Lansing
from dizzying heights.

The ride was fantastic,
but *where* were we going?
We sped ever onward
with no signs of slowing.

"Lake Michigan, next,"
said the train's engineer.
"Make room for the creatures
who'll swim aboard here."

SPLASH!

And just as he said it,
he slammed on the brake,
and we fell through the air,
splashing into the lake!

LAKE MICHIGAN

We soon left the lake for
another strange stop:
up a really tall tower,
on the side...near the top!

Boyne Mountain was next,
where the big ogres dwell,

then down in old sewers
(oh, the sewer-folk smell!).

As we raced to our next stop
the train turned too fast,
and I saw, through the window,
a **pumpkin** *whizz* past!

The ghosts started howling.

"What happened?" I said.

"We're doomed!" cried a witch.

"That's the engineer's head!"

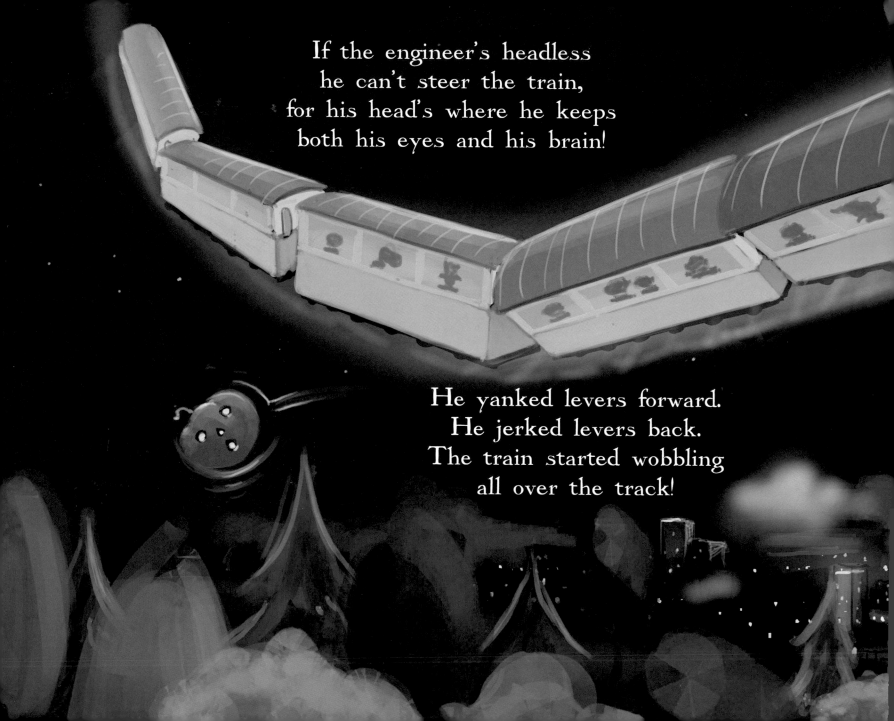

If the engineer's headless
he can't steer the train,
for his head's where he keeps
both his eyes and his brain!

He yanked levers forward.
He jerked levers back.
The train started wobbling
all over the track!

We swerved around buildings.
We darted past trees.
The speed of the turns
made us weak at the knees.

While everyone panicked,

I stood up and said,

"With the help of some friends,

we can go get that head!"

"Miss Witch," I said calmly,

"your broom, if I may?

Miss Spider, Miss Dragon,

let's go save the day!"

The engineer's head was in
Clear Lake State Park.
"Miss Dragon," I said,
"will you light up the dark?"

We twirled it around,
threw it over the top,
and we pulled the head free with a

SQUELCH and a POP!

Then back we all flew,
through the wind and the rain,
with the pumpkin containing
the engineer's brain.

With his head in our hands,
we jumped back on the train,
and we stuck his head onto
his shoulders again!

He pulled a few levers.
The ghost train slowed down.
Do you know where we were?!
We were back in

OUR
TOWN!

The ghosts started howling,
(this time with delight!),
and the gnomes hugged an alien
(a little *too* tight!).

The wizards shot sparks
that were orange and green,
and they cried, "Well done, children!
You've saved Halloween!"

"We'd be *stuck* on this train,
had you not been so daring!
But now we can stop in each town
and go *scaring!*"

We jumped off the train,
none the worse for our fright.
This had certainly been
the **best** Halloween night.

The train started moving.
Its large pistons hissed.
It circled around us
on train tracks of mist.

It launched itself skyward.
Its loud whistle blew,
and the sound that it made
was a *friendly...*

Happy Halloween